Guinea Pigs Add Up

1 2 3 4 5 6 7 8 9 10 11

Guinea Pigs Add Up

15 16 17 19 20

18

Margery Cuyler

illustrated by Tracey Campbell Pearson

Walker & Company
New York

1 2 3 4 5 6 7 8 9 10 11

First published in the United States of America in July 2010 by
Walker Publishing Company, Inc., a division of Bloomsbury Publishing, Inc.
Visit Walker & Company's Web site at www.bloomsburykids.com

For information about permission to reproduce selections from this book, write to
Permissions, Walker BFYR, 175 Fifth Avenue, New York, New York 10010

Library of Congress Cataloging-in-Publication Data
Cuyler, Margery.
Guinea pigs add up / by Margery Cuyler ; illustrated by Tracey Campbell Pearson.
p.   cm.
Summary: Mr. Gilbert brings in a guinea pig as a class pet, but it looks so lonely he brings another,
and before long the class is getting an unexpected lesson in addition—and a very full cage.
ISBN 978-0-8027-9795-7 (hardcover) • ISBN 978-0-8027-9796-4 (reinforced)
[1. Stories in rhyme. 2. Guinea pigs—Fiction. 3. Pets—Fiction. 4. Reproduction—Fiction. 5. Schools—Fiction.
6. Addition—Fiction. 7. Humorous stories.] I. Pearson, Tracey Campbell, ill. II. Title.
PZ8.3.C99Gui 2010   [E]—dc22   2009028788

Art created with pen and ink, watercolor, and acrylic gouache
Typeset in Missy BT
Book design by Nicole Gastonguay

Printed in China by Hung Hing Printing (China) Co., Ltd., Shenzhen, Guangdong
2 4 6 8 10 9 7 5 3 1 (hardcover)
2 4 6 8 10 9 7 5 3 1 (reinforced)

All papers used by Walker & Company are natural, recyclable products
made from wood grown in well-managed forests. The manufacturing processes
conform to the environmental regulations of the country of origin.

Mr. Gilbert tells our class
that soon we'll have a pet.
A garter snake? A hermit crab?
We wonder what we'll get.

On Monday, when we come to school,
a cage is by the wall.
Inside it is a guinea pig
curled up into a ball.

We cuddle him, we stroke him,
he twitters, churrs, and tweets.
He nibbles on our fingers
and eats up all our treats.

We put him back inside his cage;
he huddles on his shelf—
he looks so sad and lonely
crouching by himself.

We ask our teacher nicely
to go back to the vet
and pick another guinea pig
to play with our new pet.

Mr. Gilbert brings one back—
it turns out it's a she—
and two weeks later in the cage,
one pig gives birth to three.

Now . . . we have five guinea pigs;
we watch them use a slide

and pop-pop-popcorn on the rug,
then scuttle off and hide.

We take them to the playground—
they scamper on the grass;

we roll some rubber balls to them,
and giggle as they pass.

1 2 3 4 5 6 7 8 9 10 11

12 13 14 15 16 17 18 19 20

Then—uh-oh—eight weeks later,
five pets have fifteen more.
We count them—one to twenty;
help—guinea pigs galore!

Mr. Gilbert starts to cry,
"They really have to go!
The cage is just not big enough
to hold the overflow!"

He calls up all our parents.
"Please, please adopt our pigs;
I must find homes for all of them
before they get too big!"

My mom and dad agree
that I can take one home.
The patchy pig's my favorite,
the one I want to own.

Kaitlyn adopts the littlest;
Wayne, the waviest one.
Sophia, the pig with freckles
that's always on the run.

GUINEA PIGS SUBTRACT!!

20 - 1 = 19

20 - 2 = 18

20 - 3 = 17

20

20 - 5 = 15

20 - 6 = 14

11 10 9 8 7 6 5 4 3 2 1

Soon they're all adopted;
no pigs are left to add.

The cage looks very empty,
and we are kind of sad.

Then our teacher tells us
that yesterday he met
a rabbit sweet as honey—
now he's our classroom pet!

We name him Mr. Whiskers,
but—uh-oh—then we see

his belly growing rounder . . .

so . . .